To: Isla

Rhyming Roshumba

S Rodgers.

www.nubianamedia.com

Rhyming Roshumba

There will always be times,
When things don't go as expected.
Stay positive and persevere.
Please don't feel dejected.

-Samantha Rodgers

Roshumba was an ingenious child,
Who liked to spend her time,
Writing phenomenal poems,
And creating clever rhymes.

Wherever Roshumba went,
Her pen was by her side.
With her trusted notebook,
She was always satisfied.

Roshumba could never explain,
Why she rhymed so well.
Her talent was simply amazing,
Like a wondrous, magical spell.

Roshumba's rhymes were clever,
She delivered them with ease.
She made it look so effortless,
As if rhyming was simply a breeze.

So she entered a poetry slam,
And was confident of her poetic rhymes,
Hoping that her stage performance,
Would be utterly sublime.

She practised with her parents,
She practised on her own.
She practised her use of expression,
With a variety of endearing tones.

But on the day of the poetry slam,
She started to have concerns.
Her nerves came to the surface,
And her stomach started to churn.

Her parents gave her a cuddle,
To keep her nerves at bay,
And reassured dear Roshumba,
That everything would be okay.

As her name was announced,
She anxiously stepped onto the stage,
With all eyes upon her,
She felt like an animal trapped in a cage.

She reluctantly started her poem,
But things took a turn for the worse.
Roshumba suddenly froze,
And could not remember her verse.

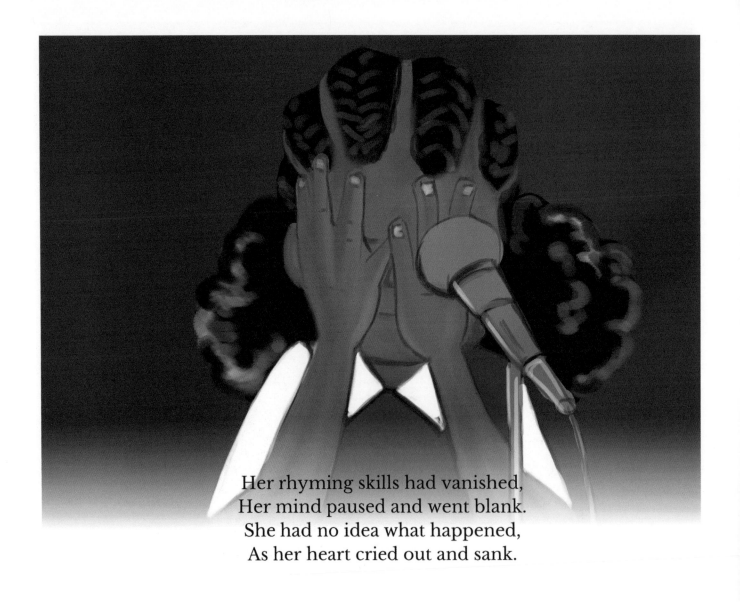

Her rhyming skills had vanished,
Her mind paused and went blank.
She had no idea what happened,
As her heart cried out and sank.

She stared into the audience,
Her mind was in a haze.
Then looked towards her parents,
And received their encouraging gaze.

She remembered what they had told her,
As her eyes welled up with tears,
That it was okay to make mistakes,
And to always face her fears.

They instilled in her that challenges,
Were simply just a test,
And that things would all work out,
If she always tried her best.

She took a long, deep breath,
And held her head up high.
She regained her composure,
And bravely waved her nerves goodbye.

Her rhymes returned with a vengeance,
As she smiled and started again.
She performed with such tenacity,
And was back in her rhyming lane.

The audience were truly hypnotised,
By her charm and humble stance.
And despite her rocky start,
She held them in a poetic trance.

When her poem was finished,
She received a rapturous standing ovation,
As the audience truly admired,
Her resilience and determination.

Roshumba cherished that day,
And the lesson that she learned,
That whenever there are difficulties,
They can always be overturned.

Roshumba is truly inspirational,
And always shares her tale,
About the poetry competition,
So that others can prevail.

She continues to write her rhymes,
And if she ever forgets,
Any lines from her poems,
She stays calm and never frets.

She is still a poetic genius,
And whenever things get tough,
She remembers her parents' wise words,
'Your best is always enough.'

Printed in Great Britain
by Amazon